Shalon

R A Campbell

Cover, cover art, and interior design by:
BDDesign – www.lulu.com/BDDesign

ISBN: 978-0-6151-5629-3

Printed in the United States of America via Lulu Press
(www.lulu.com)

For everyone who ever
encouraged me in my writing

Chapter One: Adventure

Shalon spread her wings and took flight. It had been a long time since she had used this form, and, as a result, her flight was a little shaky. However, she managed to maintain her speed and the more time she spent in her natural form, the easier it became.

Using her Mindpower, she searched for signs of life. Finally, she found a cave that had many inhabitants. Fearing that they might panic at the sight of a dragon, Shalon changed to her human form. And fell. She kept forgetting that when she changed she could not fly, unless it was the form of a flying creature that she took.

Luckily, she landed in some bushes; the soft leaves giving her a nice, cushioned landing. She was still hidden in the bushes when she saw a creature exit the cave. It was very large. Not when compared to a dragon, but when compared to the human form she now occupied, the creature was huge. The creature was very stupid, too. She could hear it as it talked to itself.

"Dumbbell good ogre. Dumbbell not smart. I just as stupid and ugly as others. Why Cookoo no love Dumbbell?"

Shalon now knew what the creature was, having known about ogres for most of her life. She had never known any that could speak more than a few syllables at one time, though. This one must be special. She wondered what she should do next. She decided to read its mind.

"Good...Ate...Cookoo...Bush...Ten...Rock..."

Shalon was confused. She wondered if she had missed part of the thoughts. It had never happened before, but then, she had never attempted to read the mind of an ogre before. Then she realized. The thoughts of ogres never made sense, even to themselves. That was part of what made them so stupid. At least she now knew that it was not a problem with her powers.

Shalon decided to look for other forms of life. She became a dragon again and took flight. The ogre just stood there, dumbfounded, staring up into the sky after her. She ignored him and flew towards the mountains. Elves lived in those mountains, as did gnomes. Shalon knew this from her studies. She did not, however, know that dragons also lived in the mountains.

The mountains loomed in front of her. Upon landing, she shifted to elf form. However, this was her first time ever trying to take such a form, so she had to work her way into it. First, she became human, because that was a form she knew well. Then elongated her ears, making them pointed like those of the elves. She thinned her face and made her chin a little more pointed. Then, she shortened herself to the proper height for elves. Finally, she subtly enhanced the pigmentation of her body: Her hair turned green, her eyes were now violet, and her skin had a greenish hue, as well.

Her father had been an elf. He had seduced her mother when she was in her human form. No one had known for certain if humans and elves could produce offspring together, but most had assumed that it would be possible. How was her father to know that her mother was really a dragon in disguise?

Shalon had never met her father, but her mother had told her about him when she was younger. Shalon was a very unique creature, being the only dragon/elf crossbreed. Her parentage had given her abilities that were normally only associated with either dragons or elves. In addition, she appeared to have some powers that neither species had.

She was a complete shape-shifter. Her mother had told her it must be because of elfin magic. Dragons were capable of using two forms – human and draconian. It had been this way for many generations now. Elves were also partial shape-shifters. Besides their inherent elf form, they were each capable of mastering three other forms, though most of them never bothered. Their natural forms seemed to be enough for them. However, there were elves that took advantage of this ability. They used their other forms to aid them in spying, hunting, traveling, and a few other purposes.

As far as she was concerned, the fact that she could use both elfin and draconian magic was what mattered, not the reasons why she had these abilities. It had certainly been useful to her in the past. Besides, at this point in time, she had more important things on her mind.

She spotted a cave and ran to it. She entered cautiously, aware that elves often used different means of guarding their homes. Another elf was standing a few feet from the entrance. She realized that he must be a guard, and froze in place. She had no idea what to do next.

"Who goes there?" demanded the guard.

"I… I do. My name is Shalon. I need a place to stay. I am an elf, like you. Please, can I stay here?" Shalon asked.

"Move into the light," the guard ordered. "I want to see you to be certain you are what you claim to be. There are rumors that there is a dragon in the area, and all humans will be turned away. Now, come forward."

Shalon did as she had been told. The elf stared at her for a while. She locked away her dragon thoughts, just before she felt the elf probing her mind. Carefully, she extended her own Mindpower in an effort to take control of his mind. She had spent years developing and enhancing her Mindpower until she was certain it was stronger than that of any elf. He felt her presence and tried to stop her, but it was too late. She was in control.

"You will let me pass and then you will forget my existence," she told him in a low but forceful voice. He was quick to obey. As soon as she was out of sight, she was literally out of his mind. Just as she had ordered, he had forgotten her completely.

Shalon continued deeper into the mountain. Eventually, she made it to the actual elfin town. Mountain dwelling elves always placed their towns in the center of the mountain, where they would have the most protection. The elves had used Mindpower to fashion the solid rock into a suitably inhabitable environment. However, that had been centuries ago, when elves were at the height of their power, and their Mindpower was much greater than the current generations could even hope to achieve.

Shalon discovered, quite by accident, that her own Mindpower was greater than that of the entire clan of elves living in this mountain. An elf came toward her and she stopped. He grabbed her and threw her against the wall, intending to knock her unconscious, no doubt so that he would be able to pursue other activities without any arguments or complaints from her. Shalon reacted instinctively, unaware until later what she had done.

Using her Mindpower, she had simultaneously transformed the rocky wall into a cushion-like substance that allowed her to remain standing and unhurt, while also causing the floor to rise in a circle around her attacker, completely closing him off from the rest of the area. This use of Mindpower, as well as the shifting of the rock, did not go unnoticed.

Elves appeared from all directions. Shalon didn't know what to do. She didn't want to enclose them in rock as well, but there seemed to be no other option. She stood against the wall, which was now solid rock again, and desperately tried to come up with an alternative. The angry elves were coming closer. Shalon panicked, and instead of thinking, she just acted. She disappeared. In her place stood a roaring dragon.

Shalon was very cramped in the cavern that, just seconds before had seemed so large. However, she would accept the discomfort easily, as her transformation had caused the elves to turn and flee, screaming in terror. She crawled desperately toward the exit. Elves scattered in front of her, clearing a path in their panic. She took to the sky as soon as she was able. She soared above the clouds, and then transformed again. This time, she became a beetle so as to be invisible from the ground. She then made her way to the other side of the mountain.

When she had gotten to the other side of the mountain, she spotted a dragon. She slowed her flight and extended her Mindpower, attempting to identify it. It was her uncle, Kaylor! She became a dragon, and Kaylor recognized her immediately.

"Shalon!" he cried. "I am very surprised to see you. What are you doing here? Where is your mother?" He landed at the entrance to his lair and she joined him. They switched to human form, and entered the cave. Kaylor could tell that something was wrong, and he asked Shalon to tell him.

"M-mother was kidnapped by a wizard!" cried Shalon. "He took her to his castle somewhere on Mirror Island! I am trying to find someone to help me save her. The wizard destroyed the village where mother and I had been living. She and I were the only two who survived. The wizard... He was obviously very powerful, because he trapped her in her human form. I..." She lowered her head, and Kaylor could see the tears falling from her face. "I fled," she whispered.

"It's okay," said Kaylor as he wrapped his arms around her and attempted to comfort her. "You did the right thing. If this wizard was able to catch your mother, then there was, in all likelihood, nothing that you could have done to help. You would only have ended up captured yourself. Or worse."

"But... She is gone now!" sobbed Shalon.

"It's okay. If you hadn't escaped, then who would have been able to tell me? No one would have known you were gone."

"I... I guess," she replied. He held her in his arms for a few minutes before he gently released her. She looked up at him.

"Do you know the name of the wizard? It could be very important," said Kaylor as his eyes darkened.

"No. I never did find that out," she told him, hanging her head again. Then, suddenly, she looked back up at him. "I overheard someone saying that he was the oldest of all wizards, though. Does that help?"

Kaylor stared at her in disbelief. He tried to say something, but when he opened his mouth, no sound escaped. Shalon stared at him expectantly. After a moment, she gave up on waiting for him to answer. She used her Mindpower to enter his mind and discover what he was thinking. She shrieked and fell to the floor as she learned the secret. Kaylor knelt next to her, taking her into his arms. He knew that she could not understand. He held her as he explained.

"About a hundred years ago, an evil wizard known as Zanthorn transformed a female dragon into a human woman. The woman fled the wizard, and managed to conceal her identity. Believing that she was now human forever, she settled into her new life. Soon, she met a man with whom she fell in love. They married, and she felt as though she wouldn't mind being human for the rest of her life after all. Her pregnancy seemed to confirm that she was, indeed human.

"When the woman went into labor, however, she went through a drastic change. She transformed into a dragon again. She delivered the baby, which was human. Or, so it was believed at the time. The woman, who was now a dragon again, was terrified. She wished, with all of her might, that she were human again. Suddenly, she was. No one believed the midwife when she told her stories of how the woman had become a dragon, and she was driven out of the village.

"As the child grew, though, she showed signs of being different from the other children. That child was Sharnelle, your mother. She discovered that she had the ability to switch from human to dragon and back again. Her mother was the same way, though she managed to conceal it better. When she was three years old, Sharnelle was playing in the yard, when another child started picking on her. After a couple of failed attempts to get the child to stop, Sharnelle lost her temper and became a dragon. She just meant to scare him, but…

"After the boy had been killed, Sharnelle and her mother were forced to leave the village. They fled for their lives, switching to their draconian forms and taking flight. Sharnelle, being so young, had difficulty at first, but she quickly learned what she needed to do, and was able to keep up with her mother.

"They came here, to these mountains, where Gendarr, your grandmother, met Flaxtor. Flaxtor is my father. He was killed when I was three, and Sharnelle, though she was only eight at the time, became my hero. I followed her everywhere. One day, she showed me her human form. She explained how she shifted form, and I tried it. As it turned out, I was able to shift form, too.

"When Sharnelle was 18, she left the mountains, to see what it was like to live as a human. I was very upset by this, and wanted to go with her, but…"

"But what?" asked Shalon.

"But mother was pregnant. It was, up until that moment, unheard of for a dragon to be pregnant, as that is not the way that we reproduce. She needed my help to keep the pregnancy hidden. I couldn't abandon her; not even for Sharnelle. When mother gave birth, however, it killed her. She had delivered four dragons, all of whom were male.

"It was up to me to determine if they, too, had the ability to change form. Two of them were able to shift quite easily, but it looked as though the other two might not have that ability. Just as I was ready to give up on them, though, they managed to change form. As soon as they were able, they left.

"It was another thirty years before I learned anything more about them. I had discovered that they had each been mating with both humans and dragons, producing more offspring than I had thought possible. However, that is how the shape-shifting dragon came into being.

"It was then that I decided I had to find your mother. I searched for quite some time before I discovered that she had caught the eye of Zanthorn, who had used his powers to make her submit to his advances. He was tying to create an heir for himself. I was able to free her, but not before Zanthorn managed to impregnate her." He hung his head, as if still ashamed that he was not able to free Sharnelle sooner. Then, he raised his face again so that he could look at her. His eyes sparkled.

"You are the result of that pregnancy," he said with a smile. Then, as he continued, his mood darkened, and the sparkle left his eyes. "When you were born, we discovered that Zanthorn was really an elf. He had been using magic to make himself appear to be human. So, you see… He is not only the oldest wizard, he is also the most powerful." His gaze fell to the floor again. Shalon opened her mouth to speak, but she was too shocked to form words. Kaylor suddenly looked up at her, with hope gleaming in his eyes. "Unless… Unless you are actually stronger than he is?"

No question had ever scared her as much as that one did. She knew that her Mindpower was stronger than that of any normal elf, but she had never expected to discover a wizard in her ancestry. She had always just assumed that the draconian magic had enhanced her own elfin abilities. At least the things she had picked up when she had read Kaylor's thoughts made some sense to her now.

She and her uncle came to the decision that she should find out just how powerful she was. They immediately set out to find a wizard who could tutor Shalon. It wasn't easy, but they found one who was willing to train her. It didn't take long to discover that she was more powerful than her teacher was. Despite the fact that they were certain she had at least as much power as her father, she still wasn't certain she wanted to put that information to the test.

She discovered more powers than she had ever imagined that she possessed, and with the help of several wizards, she learned to control and to enhance her abilities. She studied for what seemed like years, though everyone else assured her it had been days. Finally, she was ready to try to rescue her mother. She just hoped that her studies had not taken too long.

Carefully, Shalon made her way to Mirror Island, and searched for the place where her mother was being held. Keeping herself hidden, she used her Mindpower to locate her mother. Then, she planned the escape. She got as much information as possible from her mother and, using her mother's help, she managed to teleport into the cell where her mother was being held.

"Shalon!" her mother cried in a low voice. "I am so glad to see you!" The two of them hugged. Then, Shalon transformed her mother into a flea. She transformed herself into a bird, and allowed her mother to nestle between her feathers. Then, Shalon simply flew out of the cell. When she got to the mountains, she switched to her draconian form. Her mother became a human, riding on her back. Sharnelle was about to become a dragon, too, when she realized that they were already near Kaylor's lair. Shalon landed.

"Your powers are far greater than I had thought," Sharnelle said after Shalon had become human again. She hugged her daughter again. After a moment, Shalon pulled away.

"It's not over yet," Shalon said. "It won't be long at all before Zanthorn is after us. I shall have to go back and give him something else to think about." Before her mother or uncle could object, she was gone.

Sharnelle stood where she was, staring at the empty space where her daughter had just been. Then, she sighed and turned to Kaylor. Kaylor just smiled at her and continued with his daily routine. Sharnelle followed him around for a few minutes, and then said: "I wonder what she will do."

"I have no idea," admitted Kaylor. "That child is crazy, and very stubborn, and not very open about what she is plotting... She is just like you used to be!"

"I... I am not stubborn!" said Sharnelle as she glared at her half-brother.

"No, of course not," he said as he rolled his eyes. "Although, I must admit... It was odd seeing her alone like that. I never thought I would see the day she wander more than half a mile from your side."

"Well, she is in her forties now..." said Sharnelle, shaking her head sadly. "They just grow up so fast."

"Yeah, I guess so," replied Kaylor.

Chapter Two: Distraction

Shalon appeared, in a boat, about two miles from Mirror Island. She was in the elf form she had used not so long ago. However, she hoped that this time, things would work out better for her. Besides learning what abilities she had, she had also learned the control that she had lacked back then. She considered herself for a moment, and then shook her head. Her hair grew until it hung below her waist. She then enhanced her figure to make sure that an old wizard would be tempted.

Zanthorn stared into his magical pool as the boat made its way closer to his island. He waited a moment, and the picture became clearer. He could now see that there was a lone figure in the boat. Using his own magic, he caused the picture to enlarge, so he could see the figure more clearly. There was just something about this creature that made him want to know more. Her violet eyes, so cold and distant, held him in place for a long time. He decided that he must have her!

Forgetting about his captive, he set out to meet the elf from the pool. He approached cautiously, not wanting to scare her. He watched as her boat came close to the shore. She jumped out and pulled it up onto the beach. The clothing that she was wearing hardly covered anything, and Zanthorn was totally mesmerized by her beauty. Finally, he stepped out into the open, and spoke.

"Hello! And welcome," he said in a loud, but soothing voice. She jumped and turned to face him.

"Oh!" she cried out. Then, she calmed herself. "I... I didn't know that anyone was here. Uh... Where am I, anyway?" she asked politely.

"This is Mirror Island," explained Zanthorn. "And, I have lived here for a very long time."

"Mirror Island?" she squealed. "Oh! I like the sound of that! Oh... Where are my manners? Let me introduce myself. I am Temptra."

"Nice to meet you, Temptra. I am Zanthorn."

"Um... I hate to sound rude, but I am a bit desperate... Can I stay here for a while?" she asked timidly.

"Of course. You may stay in my castle. There is plenty of room there. Here, let me help you," he offered as he reached out and grasped her arm gently. He led her up the path toward the castle. "I hope that we can get to know each other and become close friends."

"Well, I am sure we will get to be very close," she said as she winked at him. "Who knows? We may even find that we have a lot in common. So... Um... Please don't think I am being rude, but... Why do you live out here all alone, Zanthorn?"

"Oh, no... That is not rude at all," he replied, smiling at her. He moved his hand to the small of her back. "The truth is, I chose to live out here. You see... I am not all that I appear to be. I am a wizard, but..." He indicated himself. "I am also an elf." He transformed into his natural form, and her eyes widened. "Elves, though they possess magic of their own, tend to frown on the magic used by wizards. Therefore, I could not stay with the elves, because I am a wizard. And, I could not stay with the wizards, because I am an elf. It was better for me to just come and live here. I hope that this will not be a problem for you."

"Me? Oh, no. It is definitely not a problem for me. You see... I am not exactly all I appear to be, either," she told him.

"Really," he said as he looked at her again. "I don't see anything wrong. What could your problem be?"

"Well," she said uncertainly. She was clearly concerned about something, but Zanthorn couldn't imagine what it might be. "I am not sure you will like my secret," she added, looking down at the ground. Then, she looked back up at him. "But, since you showed me your secret, I suppose it is only fair that I show you mine. Please, step back a moment."

"Please don't hate me," she told Zanthorn as he stepped back. She closed her eyes and swallowed. Zanthorn watched. Suddenly, Temptra was gone! In her place was a very repulsive ogress. The ogress opened its eyes and looked at him. Zanthorn's jaw dropped as he recognized the eyes that stared into his. She became an elf again, and hung her head. She turned away from him, and started walking back toward the beach. "I... I understand," she told him. He could tell she was crying. "I will leave."

"No!" he cried. "I... I admit I was shocked, but... I would really like it if you stayed."

14

"R-really?" she asked between her sobs. She stopped walking and turned back to face him. He walked up to her and embraced her. He held her in his arms for a moment, caressing her hair and telling her that things were okay. She leaned in to him and kissed him on his cheek. They headed back up to the castle.

"Wow!" Temptra exclaimed as they entered the castle. "This is amazing! It's so big! And... You live here all by yourself?"

Her question made him remember his captive. He wondered what he should do. He led her to a spare room, and told her that it was to be hers for as long as she was willing to stay. Then, under the pretext of finding some food, he left her to check on his prisoner. He was shocked to discover that the cell was empty. Then, he shrugged.

"Oh well," he muttered. "I don't need her any longer anyway. Temptra will do just as nicely, and I don't think I will have to force her into anything."

＊

As the days passed, Zanthorn and Temptra grew closer. They had told each other about their lives, and each had been sympathetic, having gone through something similar. They talked of magic, which Temptra found fascinating. It soon became very clear that Zanthorn was in love with Temptra, though they had never done anything more intimate than hugging, with the one exception of the kiss Temptra had given him on the day she had arrived. One night, Temptra asked Zanthorn if he would take her for a walk around the island. He quickly agreed.

They left the castle, and strolled along the coastline. On one side of the island there were open beaches, but on the other side, there were high cliffs that overlooked the water. As they walked along these, Temptra tripped and fell over the edge. As she hit the water, she transformed into a fish and swam away. Then, when she felt she had gone far enough, she jumped out of the water. As she left the water, she transformed into a bird and headed back to the island.

Zanthorn stood on the cliff, staring down into the water. Then, he screamed. He fell to his knees and cried into the night, declaring his love for her. After a few minutes, he calmed. He stood up and raised his arms into the air. He said an incantation. He was summoning her back to him. She fought his magic for a few moments, and then, as an idea entered her mind, she teleported herself back to the water, resuming the form of Temptra.

Her body rose through the water, buoyed by Zanthorn's magic. She was lifted up into the air, and she floated, as though weightless, up to the top of the cliffs. When she was directly across from Zanthorn, she transformed into a dragon. He stared in disbelief as Shalon opened her mouth and enveloped him in flames. He screamed. But, his screams were not of pain. They were screams of frustration. Suddenly, he disappeared. Shalon looked around, trying to find him.

A dragon appeared in the air behind her. It spewed gas from its mouth. The cloud of poison grew and floated right at Shalon. Spreading her wings, she flew upwards in a giant circle, coming back to the level of the cliffs beside the new dragon. She reached out and clutched its throat. As her claws began crushing its neck, it turned and stared into her eyes. She stared back. Suddenly, the dragon was gone again. Shalon saw Zanthorn standing on the cliffs. She flew down and landed nearby.

"You..." said Zanthorn as she became a human. "You are my daughter! I... I thought you were dead! Sharnelle had told me that you were." He lowered his eyes, staring down at his feet. His voice held no anger when he spoke again. "I suppose I had that coming, though. After all I had done..." He looked back up and stared into her eyes. There was anger in both his eyes and his voice as he hissed: "Go ahead and kill me, daughter!"

His words cut through her harder than anything she had ever experienced before. She realized, for the first time, that she had actually been trying to kill her own father. The thought sickened her. What had she become? She dropped her gaze, confused by what she was feeling. The anger was still there. The need for revenge was there as well. And yet... There was something that kept her from being able to act. She looked up at her father, and saw that he did not have such reservations. She could see the hatred in his eyes, and knew she had to do something. She lashed out at him with her Mindpower.

She filled his mind with the love she felt for her mother and uncle. She also sent him all of the wonder she felt when she was discovering new things, from plants and animals to new experiences. All of her pleasant and happy memories flowed from her to him, while he was fighting it by sending her every bad memory and thought he could manage. The two of them were shifting forms as they felt emotions and recalled memories that were not their own. The magic was affecting them in a way that they could never have imagined. Their minds merged.

This was more than either of them could handle. Both bodies shifted endlessly from one form to another, trying to find something that would contain the power of the mind that now occupied both bodies. The mind and bodies were rejecting each other. The power of the mind was so great that it caused both Shalon and Zanthorn to release their magic. The cliffs crumbled into the water. As they fell, so did the bodies. Whatever they had done with their magic, it had worked. The minds separated, and everything went dark.

Chapter Three: Problem

Shalon awoke with a start. Something was wrong, but her thoughts were still clouded, and she wasn't able to determine exactly what was happening. She was having trouble breathing. Nothing seemed to be in focus. She struggled to calm herself enough to get a grip on the situation. Her lungs felt as though they were on fire. Slowly, her vision cleared a little. She realized that she was underwater!

Shalon fought her way to the surface, moving quickly. She was in dragon form, and as soon as she broke the surface, she continued to rise up into the air, gasping for breath. When she was completely out of the water, and had managed to get her breathing under control again, she looked down at the water, discovering that there was an elf below her, swimming toward the shore.

Shalon cleared her mind and tried to reach out with her Mindpower, to find out what was going on. She gasped and opened her eyes wide with shock as she discovered that her Mindpower was gone. Panic-stricken, she looked down at the elf, and was not surprised to see that it was Zanthorn.

Questions flooded into Shalon's mind: Did he still have his powers? Was all of this part of his plan? Was he after her powers all along? And, if so, why was he not using his magic now? Then, the answer came to her. He didn't have his magic anymore, either! She swooped down and lifted him from the water. She took him to the shore, and then landed next to him.

"Is your magic gone as well?" asked Zanthorn as he stared up at her. She just looked at him for a moment. Finally, she decided that there was no harm in talking to him. She opened her mouth to speak, and realized that he would not be able to understand her if she used draconian speech. Without thinking, she shifted to human form. Both of them were caught by surprise. After a moment, Shalon spoke:

"Yes, I am afraid so. The only power I now possess is to switch forms between dragon and human."

"I see," said Zanthorn with a nod. "And, I seem to be limited in power to the basics for elves: limited Mindpower, and the ability to shift between only four forms."

"Four?" asked Shalon.

"Yes. Elf, human, ant, and bird." He was silent for a moment, as if he wanted to say something, but was not certain if he should. Finally, he spoke to her again. "I do not understand any of this." The admission shocked Shalon, and she could tell that it pained him to admit that he was not in control of the situation.

"I..." she said. She wanted so much to be able to tell him that she had the answer, but she knew that she did not have a clue what was happening, either. "I have no idea, either," she finally admitted. Zanthorn studied her for a moment, and then nodded again.

"Come, Shalon. We shall check my books, and see if we can find out what is happening, and what to do about it." He looked as if he were trying to smile at her, but couldn't quite make it work. He sighed deeply. "I do not believe that my books will be that helpful. However, I know of nothing else that we could try."

"I see," said Shalon. She reached out and took his arm. "Let's get started then." The two of them started walking toward Zanthorn's castle, unaware of the changes that were taking place all around their world.

Plants and animals were mutating and shifting forms at random. Time seemed to have been affected, as well. Things grew older or younger at random. Creatures and plants were also merging, creating entirely new beings. Nothing like this had ever happened before, and so none of the creatures of the world were prepared for it. Most were shocked to discover that they were now trapped in foreign forms. A few, however, adjusted quickly, and even seemed glad to be in their new forms.

Chapter Four: Searching

Sharnelle, now a nymph, cried out in shock. She looked around desperately. Her brother seemed to have completely disappeared. She closed her eyes and concentrated, hoping that she would still be able to communicate with him telepathically. When she discovered that she couldn't, she was disappointed, but not entirely surprised. She opened her eyes, and saw a small bird sitting on the ground in front of her, staring up at her.

"Kaylor?" she asked. The bird nodded, and flew up into the air, circling her. She held out her hand, and the bird landed on her finger. "Do you have any idea what is happening?" Sharnelle demanded. The bird shook its head furiously.

Sharnelle walked to the edge of the cliff, and surveyed the land below. There was total chaos. It seemed that she and Kaylor were not the only creatures to be affected. As she searched the area for an answer, there was a blinding flash of light. When her vision cleared, Sharnelle was certain of the problem. She just had no idea what had caused it, or what could possibly fix it.

"Kaylor," she said. "We need Shalon." The bird in her hand chirped excitedly about something, but Sharnelle could not understand what he was trying to say. "Kaylor!" she shouted. The bird was quiet, and it looked up at her. "I don't know how to speak your new language. I am glad that you can understand me, though. That makes things a little easier. Now, I need you to fly to Mirror Island and get Shalon. Use whatever means are necessary, but get her to come back with you, do you understand?" The little bird nodded. "Good. I am going to start making my way to the ocean, but in this form, it will take me a lot longer to get there. If I am not there when you get back, by all means come searching for me, okay?"

Kaylor flew into the air. He flew in circles for a short time, watching Sharnelle start her own journey. Once she was of the cliff and headed through the wilderness, Kaylor lost sight of her. He sighed and headed to Mirror Island. Being a bird was both similar to and different from being a dragon. He had to be more careful of updrafts, and predators in this form. His vision wasn't as good, either. Also, he discovered that his flights had to be much shorter than he was used to, as his new form was not able to match the speeds or distances that a dragon could manage.

As a result of all of this, it took him a lot longer to reach the ocean than he had expected. He stopped on the shore to rest. For the first time, he was actually afraid. He had never before been concerned about distances. As a dragon, he could travel halfway across the world without even considering a rest. Now, however, he was afraid that he would not be able to make it from the shore he was now on to the island where Shalon had been.

He chided himself for his fear. This was an emergency, and Shalon may be the only one who would be able to help put things right. He had to go find her, no matter what the cost. Even if the cost was his own life. Taking a deep breath, he took flight again and headed out over the ocean. He found that he was not having as much trouble flying now as he had earlier, and started to relax a little more. He looked around, realizing that he should be approaching the island.

Kaylor flew over the ocean, searching for the island. He was certain he hadn't past it, but yet, he could not find it. He gasped in horror as he realized why he couldn't find it. Mirror Island was gone!

Chapter Five: Explanation

Meanwhile, Shalon and Zanthorn were frantically searching through every book in the castle. When the last book had been searched, Shalon cried out in frustration and threw herself onto the floor. Zanthorn sighed in frustration. Then, suddenly, his eyes lit up. He remembered his magic pool. The two of them rushed into the chamber that held the pool and gazed into it.

"What is happening?" Zanthorn asked the pool. The pool did not change, and it showed nothing. Shalon reached out and lightly touched the pool with one finger. Ripples flowed outward from the point where her finger had touched the water, but they moved slowly.

"It obviously still has some magical properties," Zanthorn told her. She nodded her agreement.

"What caused this to happen?" Shalon asked. The pool grew dark, and then, as it lightened, it showed a scene. There was a dragon and an elf in the air, and a purple light surrounded them. The two creatures moved closer together and then merged. The light around them seemed to get brighter, and then it was absorbed into the creature. Then, there was a blinding flash of light, and, when they could see again, there was a ripple of purple light flowing across the scene, and the elf and dragon were falling into the water. Then, the pool went dark.

"It's worse than I suspected," said Zanthorn as he looked from the pool to Shalon. She looked up at him, not understanding what was happening. He explained it to her: "The magic that we once wielded has been freed. It will roam across the land constantly changing everything it encounters until it has been reclaimed. Unfortunately, the only ones who can reclaim it are the original owners. And…" He sighed deeply before he continued. "Since you and I are trapped *inside* it, I fear we will not be able to reclaim it."

"I refuse to believe that we are trapped," exclaimed Shalon. There is a way out of this. I am certain of that fact. We just have to find that way." She looked up at him. "Not all of the answers can just be handed to us. We have to work to figure it out."

Shalon tried to convince Zanthorn that he should not give up, but he was old and set in his ways. He had lived the majority of his life with magic, and was now too dependent upon it for him to believe he could ever survive without it. She tried to argue with him, but he refused to listen. Finally, in frustration, she stormed out of the castle. She started walking to the beach, but partway there, she changed her mind and headed the opposite direction. She was going to go back to the place where this had started.

She walked slowly but deliberately, allowing herself time to calm down. When she finally reached the point where she had jumped off the island earlier, she stared out in horror. There was no water. There was no sky. There was the edge of the island, and then there was nothing. Shalon turned away, unable to believe what she had witnessed. She turned back, looked around again, and made her decision. She deliberately stepped off the edge again, and let herself fall.

Zanthorn grabbed her wrist. He pulled her up onto the cliff again. He set her down on the ground and shook her gently.

"Shalon? Shalon, can you hear me? Oh, please don't be dead," he moaned. She did not answer him, nor did she move.

Chapter Six: Falling

Shalon was falling. She felt as though she had been falling for years. She flailed about helplessly. She was starting to regret her decision to step off the cliff. Desperately, she reached out for anything in the darkness. There seems to be nothing around her at all. She cried out, not knowing what else to do. Her screams seemed to be louder than she had thought possible.

Still reaching desperately for anything that she could hold, she continued to fall. She no longer cried out, feeling certain that this was just a waste of her time. She was starting to believe that reaching out was a waste of her time, too. Fatigue set in, and she quit reaching out. She just let herself fall, feeling nothing but despair. She hit the ground with a loud thud.

The wind had been knocked out of her, but slowly, as she struggled to breathe, she scene cleared in front of her. She was on the cliff again, but this time she was in dragon form. She looked around, and spotted the castle. She shifted to human form and approached the castle. There seemed to be something very different about it. Finally, she realized what was different. The castle looked younger! She stopped in her tracks and considered.

At first, she didn't know what she should do. Then, she decided that it was just her imagination, and she started walking again. As she approached the castle, however, she became more and more certain that this was somehow an earlier version of the castle on Mirror Island. She came around the corner, to the front of the castle, and was surprised to see a figure standing there. She almost fainted when he turned to face her.

It was a younger version of Zanthorn!

Chapter Seven: Rescue

Kaylor turned and flew back to the land. He had to find Sharnelle! Flying as quickly as he could, he retraced the flight he had taken from his home in the mountains to the beach. He didn't have to go very far before he discovered his sister, still making her way to the shore. He flew down to her and started telling her everything.

"Kaylor!" she cried. "I can't understand you! To me, you just sound like a frantic little bird. What are you trying to say?"

Kaylor flew to the ground and thought for a moment. There had to be a way for him to tell her what had happened. He looked up at her, desperately wanting her to understand what was happening. He started scratching the ground with his foot, as he tried to think of something that he could do to tell her what had happened. She knelt beside him.

"Kaylor? What are you drawing there?" Sharnelle asked him. He looked down at his foot, having just then realized what he had been doing. He looked up at her and chirped excitedly. He hopped over to an open area and started scratching the ground. After a short time, he had scratched out the word "island." Sharnelle looked at him.

"You want to tell me something about Mirror Island?" she asked. He nodded his head vigorously. "Well, what is it? What about the island?" He hopped back to the word, and scratched it out.

"It's gone?" Sharnelle shrieked. He looked up at her again and nodded. She fell the rest of the way to the ground. "I... I don't believe this!" she sobbed. She lay there and sobbed while Kaylor hopped around helplessly. He finally hopped up to her and pecked her lightly with his beak. She sat up and looked at him.

"What do we do now?" she asked as she wiped her face. "Do you have any idea?" The bird shook its head slowly. Sharnelle picked him up gently and placed him on her shoulder as she thought. "What could have happened to the island?"

Then, she jumped to her feet, dislodging Kaylor. He fell a short distance before he managed to get control and fly up to the level of her head. He stared at her, not sure what was going on. He recognized the look on her face. He knew that Sharnelle had figured something out. The smile on her face was one he had always dreaded. It was the smile she got whenever her idea would be harmful... Especially to him.

"I have an idea," she told him. "I think that you are the only one who can help us right now, Kaylor!" Her smile widened, and his heart sank a little further. This was exactly what he had feared. Her plans almost always put him in danger. "You have to find the magic that is roaming loose, and fly into it! You have to find Shalon, and hope that she will be able to fix this!"

Kaylor almost fell to the ground from the shock. It was such a simple plan, and one that he should have thought of for himself. He nodded eagerly and then flew up into the air. He searched the area, and finally found the magic, floating near a mountain. He shot toward it like a living dart. As he reached it, there was a moment of disorientation, and when his senses cleared, he was surprised to discover that he was flying above Mirror Island!

He quickly spotted two figures, and flew closer to see if he could identify them. One of the creatures held the other. He discovered that one was an elf, and the other was human. The elf was not one he recognized, however, the human was Shalon! Kaylor flew down toward the ground, realizing for the first time that he was back in dragon form.

Zanthorn, horrified by the approach of a dragon that had just appeared above him, threw himself over Shalon's body. At that same moment, something strange happened. The island began shaking, and there was an earsplitting shriek. Zanthorn turned to look up at the dragon, and the dragon stared back down at him. He realized that neither he nor the creature was responsible for the noise. The dragon, which seemed to come to the same conclusion, landed softly near Zanthorn.

The shrieking grew even louder.

Chapter Eight: Message

Shalon stared at Zanthorn. He was definitely younger, but, in a strange way, he was exactly the same. She had never encountered anything like this before. Before she could regain her composure, Zanthorn noticed her and went red with rage.

"What are you doing here, stranger?" he screamed. Shalon took a step backwards.

"I… Uh… I… I am not sure. You see… I…"

"You were not invited, and I have no use for visitors right now. If you wish to remain alive, then you must leave now!"

Shalon just stared at him. She was truly frightened by him. She had no idea what she should do. Instinctively, she reached out with her Mindpower, and was shocked again as she realized that it was working again. She tried to probe his mind, but his defenses were like no others she had ever seen. His magic was truly powerful. Finally, she withdrew her magic and looked at him.

"I came to give you a message, and I cannot leave until you have heard it," she told him.

"You will die, then!" he screamed. As he raised his hand, preparing to release a magic bolt, Shalon used some magic of her own. The bolt flew from Zanthorn's hand but instead of hitting Shalon, it appeared to pass right through her. That was a little trick that Shalon had learned while practicing her wizardry before she had come to Mirror Island. The shock on Zanthorn's face was clear. She smiled at him.

"Now are you willing to listen to the message?" she asked sweetly.

"Very well. If it will help to get rid of you, I will listen," he said. He was looking around, and Shalon could feel the rise of magic in the area. She knew that she had better tell him what he needed to know, and then get out of there.

"The one you seek is not Sharnelle. There is one even more powerful." Zanthorn was clearly interested in what she was saying. She could not believe what she was about to do. "The one you want is Shalon. She is the offspring of a dragon and an elf. She has the full powers of both. She is also adept in wizardry. If you are careful, you can take her by surprise, and capture her instead of Sharnelle. That is all." Shalon then disappeared.

She reappeared near the village where she had once lived as a human. She started to walk to the village, and then stopped. She couldn't go into the village looking like Shalon! She thought quickly, and came up with the perfect disguise. Temptra would be the one to enter the village. Once more, she headed for the village. There was an explosion, and she realized that she was now too late. Zanthorn was attacking the village. She started to run, but another explosion knocked her to the ground.

Chapter Nine: Done

Kaylor shifted to Human form after he had landed. He took a step towards the elf. He now realized that the elf must be Zanthorn. The realization made him stop. He wasn't sure what powers, if any, Zanthorn still possessed.

"What is going on?" he asked.

"Who are you?" asked Zanthorn. The shrieking grew even louder, and the two of them had to yell in order to be heard above it.

"I am Kaylor. I am Shalon's uncle," he yelled. Zanthorn nodded, and moved out of the way. Kaylor rushed to Shalon's side and knelt beside her. Zanthorn knelt on her other side.

"I... I don't know what happened to her," said Zanthorn. Before Kaylor could respond, the shrieking stopped and Shalon opened her eyes.

"It's done," she said in a harsh whisper. "It's all over now."

Zanthorn looked up at Kaylor. Kaylor seemed to be thinking the same thing. He raised his gaze to meet Zanthorn's. As their eyes met, there was a flash of purple light.

Chapter Ten: Change

Kaylor stepped outside his cave, wondering what had happened, and saw a dragon approaching. It was Sharnelle! He shifted to human form and waited as she landed and also shifted form. He reached out to hug her, but stopped when he saw the condition that she was in. He was about to speak when she broke into sobs.

"What's wrong?" he asked as he embraced her.

"Shalon has been kidnapped! Zanthorn came to the village and took her! When he first appeared, I was certain that he was there for me, but he took Shalon instead! He is holding her captive on Mirror Island by now. What am I going to do? I haven't even gotten the chance to get her a tutor for her wizardry!"

"Calm down. I was inside the magic with them. He didn't hurt her. Something happened. She was never kidnapped. You were, and she saved you. Don't you remember?"

"Kaylor, what are you talking about? I haven't been rescued! I was never kidnapped!" screamed Sharnelle.

"Oh!" exclaimed Kaylor. "She did it! She actually did it! Everything has changed now! Sharnelle, come quickly! We have to go!" He let go of his sister, took a step backward, and was about to shift to dragon form when Sharnelle grabbed him by his shoulders and started shaking him.

"Kaylor! Have you been paying attention? What is wrong with you? I just told you that Zanthorn has kidnapped my daughter! Where are you wanting me to go?"

"We are going to go to Mirror Island!" he said as he pushed her gently away. "That is the only way I can convince you of what really happened! Please, we have to hurry."

He then shifted to dragon form and took off. Sharnelle called out to him, but he refused to turn back and look at her. Finally, she shifted to dragon form and began chasing him.

Chapter Eleven: Return

Shalon woke up in a dungeon. She sat up slowly and held her head in her hands. When the pain had subsided enough for her to function again, she looked around, not only at her surroundings, but at herself as well. She discovered that she did not have any injuries. Other than a throbbing in her head, and a slight disorientation, she was fine. However, she was being held in a cell that contained only a stone slab for a bed, and nothing else. Slowly, she got to her feet.

As she stood there, wondering what was going on, a man opened the door and entered. He looked very familiar to her, as if she should recognize him, but she could not remember having ever met the man before. Before she could say anything, he had fixed her with an icy stare that seemed to bore right through her. She shuddered and took a step backwards. He smiled evilly and stepped closer to her. Her eyes widened with fright, and he stared at them for a moment, unable to speak or move.

"You!" he exclaimed. "Sharnelle has tricked me! You are my daughter!"

With that exclamation, Shalon's memories returned to her. She remembered being attacked in the village and going to find her uncle. She remembered training in wizardry and freeing her mother, only to come back to the island in hopes of distracting, and getting to know, Zanthorn. The memories were all suddenly there again, and she was finally able to explain to herself what had happened.

"No, father," she said in a timid voice. "It was not Sharnelle who tricked you. I did it. It was the only way I could save us all. We were trapped in the magic, don't you remember?" She knew that eventually his memories would return, as would Kaylor's memories, if they had not already. No one else would know, though. Only those who had been *inside* the magic would be able to remember what had taken place there.

She had managed to change the past. And, by doing that, she had created a different present, and saved her future. She looked at her father, hoping that he would remember. She saw the look on his face go from one of disbelief to one of understanding, and knew then that his memories had also returned to him. Tears fell from his eyes.

"You are free to do whatever you wish. Goodbye, daughter," he said as he disappeared. His final word echoed for an instant, and then, there was an eerie silence. The castle suddenly disappeared. Vegetation appeared in its place, and soon, she was seeing all sorts of animals roaming around. Shalon tried to understand what was happening, and when the truth finally became clear to her, she fell to the ground and started crying. She had only met her father recently, and now he was gone!

She was still crying when Kaylor and Sharnelle reached the island. They spotted her, and quickly landed, becoming human the moment they were on the solid ground. They rushed to her, and fell to their knees beside her.

"What has happened?" asked Sharnelle.

"Zanthorn is gone. Mirror Island is no more. This is now Life Island again, as it was before he came here. He was only able to remain alive as long as he had the need to create an heir. Once he discovered that I am not only his child, but also even more powerful than he ever was, he no longer had a reason to exist. That was his plan all along. I will never get to know my father," she sobbed.

"Oh, Shalon, I am so sorry," sighed Sharnelle as she held her daughter close to her. She looked up at Kaylor, uncertain what to do next. He shook his head, indicating that he didn't know what they should do now, either.

"I guess it is time for us to go home?" Kaylor suggested after a moment.

"I... I suppose so," said Sharnelle. "Are you ready to go?" she asked Shalon.

"Yes. I think I can go now," said Shalon. She leaned back from her mother and wiped her eyes. After everything she had been through, she still couldn't believe that she had lost her father so soon after getting to know him. She realized that it was the fact that she had changed the past that proved to him that she was more powerful than he was. If she had not done it, they would all have perished. Still, she wasn't sure she would have done it, if she had known the price she would have to pay.

Kaylor helped his sister and niece to their feet, and then looked around. He was amazed at how different the island looked now. He knew that Zanthorn was powerful, but had not been willing to believe that his mere presence was enough to change an island so drastically. He shook his head again and turned to look at Shalon.

"Are you sure you are ready to go?" he asked.

"Yeah," replied Shalon. "It's over now."

"Not yet, Shalon!" Shalon looked around.

"Who is that?" she asked.

"What?" asked Sharnelle.

"Who is what?" asked Kaylor.

"I..." said Shalon. "Oh, nothing. I guess I am still upset about everything that has happened. Let's go."

"I know you can hear me!" boomed the voice. Shalon cried out and grabbed her head. She looked up at her uncle, who had placed his hand on her shoulder.

"Are you okay?" he asked. She nodded and brushed his hand off. Then, inside her head, she said:

"Who are you?"

"You already know that," came the voice.

"No, I don't!" she told the voice.

"Yes, you do. We are one now," answered the voice.

"Zanthorn!" she said out loud. Sharnelle and Kaylor jumped and looked around. When they did not see him, they turned their attention back to Shalon. She swallowed the lump that had formed in her throat. Her mother and uncle stared at her, as if waiting for her to explain. She looked from one to the other, and then laughed nervously.

"Zanthorn," she said again, "is not really gone. At least, not completely." She spoke with a calm, level voice. "As long as people remember him, he will never truly be gone." She turned and took a step. "Let's go home."

"All right," said Sharnelle, in a confused voice. "If you say so."

"Let's be on our way, then," said Kaylor as he shifted to dragon form and took flight.

"You can't go home! This isn't over yet!" boomed the voice again. Shalon almost screamed, but instead, she made only a strangled cry as she fought to regain control of herself.

"Uh..." said Shalon. "You two go ahead. There... There is something that I need to do." Her mother turned and looked at her as Kaylor landed and shifted form again.

"Alone," concluded Shalon.

"Okay," said Sharnelle in a voice that betrayed her confusion. She looked at Kaylor, and then back at Shalon. Her voice was not confused when she spoke again, but hurt. "Even though I don't understand this. Even if I *am* your mother, and even if I did *give birth to you*, I will just go now, with no explanation of what is going on, if that is really what you want."

"Good! Thanks!" said Shalon as she leaned forward and kissed her mother on the cheek. Then, before Sharnelle had time to react, Shalon was gone.

"Wait! I..." called Sharnelle. Then, she hung her head and sighed. She looked up at Kaylor. He smiled at her, and she dropped her head again. Then, Kaylor started laughing and wrapped his arms around her.

"Come on, Sharnelle. Let's go home, okay?" He let her go and shifted to dragon form again. This time, when he took flight, he didn't look back. He could feel his sister's presence beside him, and knew that she was with him. He would do more to comfort her when they got back to the caves, and he was able to relax again.

Chapter Twelve: Gnarstal

Gnarstal, an ancient gnome who lived in the same mountains as the dragons, sensed a force of evil magic strong enough to destroy the entire world. His ancient bones creaked and moaned in protest as he made his way to his feet. Once he was standing, he headed for the exit. He had amazing speed and agility that no one would have guessed he possessed by looking at him.

He traveled from his home, through his village and even deeper into the mountains. He knew that he needed help in order to stop the force of evil he had sensed. There were six others that would be needed. The two dragons, Sharnelle and Kaylor, were already involved. With being older than the others needed, their wisdom would be vital to the success of the mission, since Gnarstal was not certain he would survive long enough to fulfill the prophecy.

Besides the dragons, Gnarstal also had to find Kharn, a powerful gnome who had exceeded all other gnomes in terms of magic; Reeflak, who was the queen of the fairies; Sylt, the leader of the bat-wing gargoyles; and Tanjork, the leader of the bird-wing gargoyles. Of these, the ones that Gnarstal had the most reservations about were Sylt and Tanjork, as the two types of gargoyles were at war, and may not be willing to set their differences aside, even if the fate of the entire world depended on it.

His first stop was a neighboring gnome village, where he sought out Kharn. He was told, however, that Kharn had left the village some time ago, and that no one was certain where the powerful gnome may be now. One gnome suggested that Gnarstal look for Kharn higher in the mountains, as Kharn had once stated that he would like to study the dragons. Gnarstal thanked the members of the village for their information, and headed in the direction that they suggested, hoping that he would be able to find Kharn soon.

Chapter Thirteen: Waiting

After returning to his cave, Kaylor tried to convince Sharnelle that Zanthorn really had kidnapped her, and that Shalon had freed her. Sharnelle insisted that it was all in Kaylor's head. Kaylor sighed in frustration.

"Listen to me!" he screamed. "If it really went the way you claim it did, then how did Zanthorn even know that Shalon existed? You know very well that he would not have let her live if he did not know for certain that she was your daughter. You know that as well as you know your own name! Stop deceiving yourself, Sharnelle! There is no way that your version makes any sense!"

"I hate it when you are right," said Sharnelle with a deep sigh.

"Finally!" exclaimed Kaylor as he smiled and sat down next to her. Suddenly, she sat upright and clutched his wrist. "Kaylor," she gasped. "Zanthorn isn't dead!"

"That must be what Shalon is doing, then," said Kaylor. "She spoke his name, and then convinced us to come back here while she went off to take care of him. He is more powerful than we thought! We will have to go and help her before it is too late!" He jumped to his feet. Sharnelle grabbed him and pulled him back down.

"No! We must remain here," said Sharnelle in a sad, defeated voice.

"What are you talking about?" Kaylor cried. He couldn't believe what he had just heard. "She is your own daughter!"

"Don't you think I know that?" demanded Sharnelle. "Don't you think that I *want* to help her? I would give anything just to be able to help her with this! Can't you understand? Zanthorn and Shalon are one! They probably have been since she was born! Didn't you notice the way his powers decreased when she was born? When he disappeared... He didn't die! He... Oh! Shalon is now a greater threat to Htrae than Zanthorn ever was!"

"What are you talking about?" asked Kaylor.

"Zanthorn is in Shalon's body! He may already have gained full control of it! Do you have any idea what this means? Do you realize how much danger the world is in if Zanthorn gets full control of Shalon's powers?"

"You're right," said Kaylor. He felt as though he had just been slapped.

"We... We have to find a way to destroy Zanthorn without harming Shalon in the process," said Sharnelle.

"I fear that may be impossible," said Kaylor.

"No!" screamed Sharnelle as she got to her feet. "There has to be a way, and I *will* find it!"

Chapter Fourteen: Kharn

"What does all of this mean to me?" asked Kharn.

"Well, Kharn. If you do not help, then no one will survive. Htrae will become merely an empty sphere. Certainly *that* means something to you," said Gnarstal.

"Alright," said Kharn after a moment of thought. "I will help. What do we do first?"

"We must travel to the land of the fairies and convince Reeflak to join our cause, as well. But first, we must wait for Sharnelle and Kaylor, as they are to be our transportation. At least, I hope that they will be willing to act in that capacity."

The two gnomes made a fire and waited for the two dragons to arrive. They talked about several different things before Sharnelle and Kaylor finally arrived. The two dragons landed and shifted to gnome form, which impressed Kharn and Gnarstal. Before Gnarstal was even able to open his mouth, Kharn began explaining everything. The dragons agreed to help, and also agreed to provide transportation, company, and protection for the two gnomes. Once they were back in their natural forms, the dragons waited for the gnomes to mount and then took flight. They weren't sure how long it would take to reach the land of the fairies, but they knew they had to get there as quickly as possible.

The arrival of two dragon-riding gnomes was neither a common nor welcome experience in the land of the fairies. Reeflak managed to calm her people by telling them that the arrivals had been expected. The fact that all four of the visitors were friends helped to calm the nerves of the fairy folk, though some still had their doubts as to the reasons for such an arrival. Despite any suspicions or doubts they may have had, though, the fairies welcomed the new arrivals as honored guests.

"Welcome, friends," said Reeflak. "I know already why you have come. I am almost prepared for the journey ahead. We should be able to head to the gargoyle territories in the morning. I will need to find someone to lead in my absence, and will be choosing tonight. Until that happens, though, you are free to join us. We are about to have a feast. Would you care to join us?"

"We'd be honored," said Gnarstal. He and Kharn dismounted and waited while Sharnelle and Kaylor transformed. Sharnelle was a fairy, while Kaylor chose the form of a gnome. They all enjoyed the feast, and when it was over, they began talking about their plans for the next day's journey. They were interrupted by the approach of a unicorn.

Chapter Fifteen: Struggle

Shalon was losing her battle with Zanthorn. Frantically, Shalon became a dragon in a desperate attempt to defeat her father and take complete control of her body again. It seemed to work, for the presence in her head faded. Unfortunately, though, it did not disappear altogether. Shalon knew that she needed help, but she was not able to determine what course of action would be best. Finally, she decided that she should find a place where there was no one around. At least then the rest of the world would be safe for a little while longer.

She took to the air, searching for a place where she would be able to turn all of her attention to the fight at hand, without having to think about what would happen should she lose. As she flew through the air she grew increasingly tired. She was afraid to land, but even more afraid of what would happen if she didn't. She did not want to fall asleep, because she knew that if she did, Zanthorn would take control of her body. He was dangerous enough on his own. She didn't want to think of the damage that he could cause if he had complete control over her body.

Shalon realized that she was falling and spread her wings as far as she could. She realized that she would not be able to stay awake for much longer. She needed a plan, and she needed it fast. The plan just materialized in her head as she landed. As soon as she was firmly on the ground, she changed form. This time, however, she chose something she had never chosen before. She chose a squirrel for two reasons: it was something that she was certain Zanthorn had never used before, and it was small enough that it should keep him from doing too much damage before she was able to take control again.

As soon as the transformation was complete, Shalon gave up her internal fight, and fell into the welcome abyss of unconsciousness.

Chapter Sixteen: Rirrom

All five of the creatures gathered just outside Reeflak's home assumed that the unicorn was fake. After all, unicorns hadn't been seen in several centuries. Many of the inhabitants of the world believed that the unicorns had either died off, or had never really existed at all.

"Are you a dragon?" asked Kharn, since dragons were the only creatures he knew of who could shift forms so convincingly.

"That is no dragon!" hissed Kaylor. He and Sharnelle had transformed to their natural forms when they first sighted the unicorn. "It must be some other creature in disguise! Can anyone detect an illusion spell?"

"I assure you all that I am real," declared the unicorn. "Believe me. I do not wish to be here any more than you want me to be here. I was quite content where I was. However, that is irrelevant. I am here now because a magical disturbance has created several... Gates, I suppose we could call them. They are... Portals between my world, Evol, and this world, which I believe you all call Htrae. If we do not work together, then these worlds will either become one, or they will both be destroyed. Neither of those options really appeals to me."

"What?" asked Sharnelle.

"He, or she..." began Gnarstal. He turned form Sharnelle to the unicorn. "I am sorry, unicorn. Perhaps we should start with introductions. I am Gnarstal. This other gnome here is Kharn. The two dragons," he said as he indicated each of them in turn, "are Sharnelle and Kaylor. And this is Reeflak, the queen of the fairies."

"My name is Rirrom," said the unicorn. "I am the lead mare of my herd, second in command only to the herd stallion. I was forced to leave my home world and come to this strange world in order to help you all convince the gargoyles to join in the fight against a terrible villain who lives here."

"But..." said Reeflak. "How is it that you can know so much about our world, when this is the first time we have ever heard of yours?"

"My daughter, Acire, was in her human form one day and for no apparent reason, she dropped to the ground, unconscious," said Rirrom. "Since then, she has been unable to transform, and even though she has awakened, she has said very little other than that we must help someone named Shalon defeat someone named Zanthorn. On occasion, though, she has been able to give us disjointed details about this world."

"Details?" asked Kharn. "Such as what?"

"A dragon that can not only change forms, but also has elfin magic. A quest to save Sharnelle. A destructive release of raw magical power that never really happened. A new quest, this time to save Shalon. Strange things like that. Then, the gate was discovered, and I was selected to come here to help set things right," said Rirrom. "If you are here to help, then you are more than welcome to join us. We will be leaving in the morning to seek the help of the gargoyles. Will you join us, Rirrom?" asked Reeflak.

"I want to make sure that it is clear to all of you that I am doing this for two reasons only. The first reason is that I wish to have my daughter back to the way she was, and I believe that this is the only way to achieve that. The second reason is because I want to save the world that I know and love. Once I am certain that these two things have been accomplished, I will leave. However, until then, I will do whatever I can to help. Beginning with this," said the unicorn as her horn lit up.

Chapter Seventeen: Squirrel

Zanthorn had been waiting for this moment, and was ready. Before Shalon was fully asleep, he had taken control of the body. Having been an elf his entire life, he was unaccustomed to being in many other forms. He soon discovered that before he could use magic, he had to master control of the body he now inhabited. Shalon, having been born into a race of creatures that could shift their forms at will, would not have had any difficulty changing form again. Zanthorn, however, was not Shalon, and did not have her magic, despite sharing her body.

Thoughts flooded his mind. The thoughts led to memories. Long ago, before he had moved to Mirror Island, he had mastered control of other forms. He thought about those now, wondering if there was a chance that one of them could help him with the current situation. The forms he had mastered before were ant, dragon, human and bird. None of them seemed to be helpful for the rodent form he now had. He decided that he would just start with the basics, and work from there.

He used his arms and legs. That was easy. Then, he worked on facial expressions. When he felt comfortable with all of this, he decided to work on the one thing that had worried him. The tail was a part for which Zanthorn could see no real purpose. He decided he had learned enough about this form, and started walking. He had no destination in mind, and before long he had wandered into a meadow. Suddenly, a wolf stood before him! He scrambled backwards for a couple of steps, and then turned and fled. The wolf followed. Finally, Zanthorn spotted a tree.

As the wolf grew closer, Zanthorn jumped into the air and landed on the tree trunk. He clawed his way up the tree to a branch. He looked down at the wolf below him, breathing heavily from the exertion. The wolf watched him for a couple of seconds, and then turned and left. Zanthorn sighed deeply and looked around. He could see a lot more from where he was. Deciding that the treetops were safer for him to use for travel, he started walking along the branch. And immediately fell to the ground.

He sat up, and rubbed his head. He looked up at the branch, and tried to figure out what had happened. Cautiously, he stood up and approached the tree again. He climbed it again, paying more attention to what he was doing. When he reached the branch, he studied it carefully, looking for whatever it was that had caused him to fall. There was nothing on the branch that indicated why he would have fallen. Carefully, testing his footing with each inch, he tried to walk across the branch again. He lost his balance and fell a second time.

"What is going on?" he squeaked in the language of squirrels. He looked up again, and saw another squirrel walking along a higher branch, and realized what had happened. Squirrels used their tails for balance! That is why he kept falling. Because he was not used to having a tail, he had attempted to cross the branch the way an elf or a human would. He chuckled to himself as he got up and climbed the tree for a third time. This time, when he stepped out onto the branch, his footing held, and, by using his tail, he managed to keep his balance and walk along the branch.

After walking carefully back and forth along the branch, he decided to attempt something more dangerous. He began running and scurrying along the branch, and was surprised to see how quickly he was able to adapt to using the tail, now that he knew he had to use it. Finally, he decided that he wanted to know more about being a squirrel, especially since he may never again have the chance to use this form. He took off across the branch, and when he approached the edge of it, he launched himself into the air. With a squeal of exhilaration, he grabbed onto another branch and pulled himself up onto it. He had never felt so free or active in all of his long life.

He continued his adventures among the trees for a while. He couldn't believe how much fun he was having. It had been so long since he had done anything just because of the pleasure it brought to him, and he was surprised to discover that he could have fun, given the current situation. And that realization brought the fun to a halt. He remembered what he had been in the process of doing, and stopped where he was. However, he forgot to use his tail for balance, and fell once again.

He landed on his back. He opened his eyes and stared up at the sky. His eyes moved quickly, scanning the area. Things were different. Carefully, he sat up. When he saw a dragon sleeping nearby, he gasped and jumped to his feet. Then, he realized that he was familiar with that particular dragon. It was Shalon! He looked down at himself, and discovered that he was an elf again. He also noticed that he was not wearing anything. Without thinking, he snapped his fingers and conjured his robes.

Looking around again, he decided that the place was familiar, though he was certain he had never been there before. He wondered how such a thing was possible. Then, he noticed a clearing. He walked over to it, and saw a unicorn grazing in the open space. Finally, he realized how he knew the place. He had dreamt of it! In fact, he had seen parts of it in his magic pool. His mind filled with questions, and all he knew for certain was that he was in a world known as Evol, and that, by being here, he had been freed from his connection to Shalon.

The unicorn stopped grazing and started to move away. Zanthorn decided to follow it. He shifted to the bird form he had mastered years ago, and flew into the air. From the sky, he had no problems at all spying on the unicorn. It had a bright red body with a tan mane and tail. Its hooves were silver, and its horn appeared to be made of opal. Zanthorn recognized the unicorn from his dreams. And, because of this, Zanthorn knew exactly where the stallion was headed.

Zanthorn flew ahead of the stallion and found the herd. He landed nearby. Because he had been a unicorn in his dreams, he assumed that he would be able to use the form well enough to fool the others. Concentrating on the reflection he had seen in the pool when he had been dreaming, and calling on magic he had not used in many decades, Zanthorn took the form of a unicorn. He was a pale, bluish-green with a lavender mane and tail. He stood on pink hooves and had a horn made from brilliant blue sapphire. It was only after the transformation was complete that he discovered the unicorn was female! Before he had time to react, the stallion he had been following appeared. Zanthorn knew that the unicorn standing before him was named Majyk, and that Majyk knew the form he had just taken.

"Acire!" exclaimed Majyk. His tone revealed his shock. "I was unaware that you could change form again!"

Chapter Eighteen: Sylt

When their sight returned after a blinding flash of light, the group from the land of the fairies discovered that Rirrom had transported them to the home of Sylt. They were now right beside him. Sylt, having been caught off guard, was shocked to see them, and actually fell to the floor. As he stood up, Reeflak stared at him. He was about as tall as an elf. He had icy blue skin, neon orange hair, and eyes that glowed an eerie shade of green. His wings reminded Reeflak of a bat, but somehow, these were more impressive, and, somehow, beautiful.

"Who are you, and why have you invaded my home?" demanded Sylt.

"I am Reeflak, the queen of the Fairies. I have come here, with my friends, to convince you to end your war and to help us save all of Htrae. I am accompanied by Kaylor and Sharnelle, who are dragons; Gnarstal and Kharn, who are gnomes; and Rirrom, the unicorn," she explained, pointing to each of her companions as she said their names.

"Get that horrible monstrosity out of here!" screamed Sylt. "No unicorn is allowed in *my* home!" His eyes grew darker as he spoke. The others turned to Rirrom, who disappeared without being asked. The others turned back to look at Sylt.

"What is wrong with unicorns?" asked Reeflak.

"Several years ago," began Sylt, "Well, actually, I suppose it is now going on two centuries, my son fell in love with a unicorn who had been impersonating another gargoyle. I told my son to forget about it, and just concentrate on his lessons, but he was young, only a little over a hundred at the time, and was convinced that he knew it all. He said he would not speak to me again until I had agreed to let him continue seeing his new love interest. At the time, we did not know that it was a unicorn. He locked himself in his room and refused to come out again."

"That sounds like a young one, alright," said Sharnelle. Sylt nodded and continued his story:

"A few days later, my son had kept his word. I had not seen or heard from him. I was out hunting when I happened upon the young gargoyle with whom my son claimed to be in love. I followed her, being curious as to whether or not she was worthy of my son. I saw her transform into a unicorn and return to her herd. Naturally, I came home and told my son. He became enraged, and flew away. That was the last time I ever saw him. I blamed that unicorn, and all of those like her."

"I suppose that I can understand your feelings. Even though I cannot be certain I would feel differently if something similar had happened to me, I *can* tell you that, given the dire nature of the present circumstances, I would be able to set my personal feelings aside, at least long enough to save our world. I would definitely be willing to form an alliance, no matter how unsettling it would be, with an enemy in order to save the world," explained Reeflak.

"And, I suppose that is a valid way of looking at it," said Sylt. "But, let me tell you the way *I* see it. When the world is destroyed, then so are my enemies. My memories will also be no more. My pain will finally end. From where I stand, I can see no good coming from such an alliance. I am sorry that you have wasted your time, but I am not going to help you. Bye."

And, without saying anything else, he turned and left the room. No one followed him. There was no point. Not one of them could come up with a good argument that they believed would be enough to convince Sylt to help them. They decided to leave it, for now.

Reeflak, being the most powerful one present, transported them to where Rirrom had gone when she left the home of the gargoyle. Looking around, they spotted the unicorn resting beside a pool of water. Upon seeing them, Rirrom switched to a human form, for she had not mastered, or even attempted, any of the forms of the creatures that were with her now. She was a very beautiful woman, with long peach-colored hair and lavender eyes. She wore a bright yellow dress, that matched the color of her hide when she was in her natural form.

"I think our next move should be to visit Tanjork," she said. Then, she yawned and added, "But that can wait until morning."

"So, you aren't mad?" asked Sharnelle after she had switched to human form.

"Why should I be mad?" she wondered. "And, why do you choose a human form if you hate them so?"

"The only humans left in this world are those who use the form instead of their natural ones. There are villages filled with them, and some of them have used the form for so long that they cannot even remember their natural forms. Many have only been able to use the two forms. In fact, until the recent release of magic, I had only two forms. Now, however, I have no idea how many different forms I could assume," explained Sharnelle.

"What part do you play in all of this, dragon-woman?" asked Rirrom in the coldest tone any of them had heard.

"Shalon is my daughter, and Zanthorn is Shalon's father. What does it matter to *you*, 'corn-woman?" responded Sharnelle in a tone that many would have argued was even colder than the one Rirrom had used.

"My name is Rirrom," said the unicorn.

"And mine is Sharnelle. So what?" demanded the dragon.

There was a tense silence, as no one knew what to say next. The silence was broken by the approach of a pink gargoyle with dark gray hair and glowing blue eyes. Her wings were birdlike, and covered in large, beautiful golden feathers. She had talons for feet, and when she landed, it was slightly awkward. All of the creatures that were already on the ground turned to look at her.

Chapter Nineteen: Awakening

Shalon woke to find herself at the base of a tree. Upon realizing that she was in dragon form, she assumed that she must have been dreaming. That didn't bother her at all. She marveled at the thought of being rid of Zanthorn. The land was far below her in mere seconds. Yellow clouds zoomed by at great speed as she soared through a green sky. Three moons, of a darker green than the sky itself, hung in a triangle before her.

Unable to control herself, she started flying in loops and doing other tricks she had learned when she was younger. This was the happiest she had been in weeks, and she wanted it to go on forever. After flying for some time, Shalon realized that, instead of feeling tired, she only felt even more energized.

She looked down at the forest below. It was comprised of blue trees that had red and black leaves. She was amazed at how different things were here in her dream. Water was pink instead of blue, the grass was gray, dirt was a bright white, and the few flowers she had seen were an ugly shade of brownish orange.

Without any warning, she was homesick. She wanted to be back at Uncle Kaylor's cave, with him and her mother. Suddenly, all she could think of was how wrong these colors were, and what things should really look like. The sky should have been a pale pink, and there should have been six smaller, purple moons in the sky, not three large green ones. Everything just seemed so wrong to her.

"What a strange place this is," she said as she continued her flight. Out of the corner of her eye, she noticed a line in the sky that glimmered. She was very cautious as she approached it. She had no idea what it could be, as she had never encountered anything like it before.

First, she circled around it. It didn't appear to be dangerous, so she flew closer to it. The next thing she knew, she was in a cave. She had to change form quickly to avoid being crushed. The first form that came to mind was elf, so that is the one she used. In this form, she was easily able to move around inside the cave, and her elfin eyes allowed her see clearly in the darkness. She was able to find the exit quickly enough, and she rushed out into the open air. As soon as she could see the sky, however, a net fell upon her, and gargoyles with leathery wings surrounded her.

"You are now the captive of Sylt!" hissed the leader of the gargoyles. "If you come along peacefully, then you shall live long enough to meet him. However, if you give us trouble, then you will be dead before your body even reaches the ground."

Chapter Twenty: Tanjork

"My name is Yeznull," said the female gargoyle after she had landed amongst the group. "I am in the ranks of the army of Tanjork. He demands to know what you are doing in his domain."

"We are preparing to rest for the night," explained Reeflak. "We are on a mission of peace. We would like to speak with Tanjork as soon as possible."

"And, how do I know you won't try to kill him? You could be spies of Sylt!" hissed Yeznull.

"How much do you know about Sylt?" asked Kaylor.

"I know enough," Yeznull retorted.

"Then this should be enough to convince you that we are not working for him," said Rirrom as she shifted to her natural form. Yeznull stared at the unicorn for a moment. The others could understand her shock, as they had all experienced it themselves when they had first seen Rirrom. After a moment, Yeznull recovered from her shock and eyed them all suspiciously.

"And, how do I know that this is not some sort of trick?" she wanted to know.

"Think about it. If we had wanted to harm you or Tanjork, we would have already attacked. We are not all what we appear to be," said Gnarstal.

"What do you mean?" demanded the gargoyle.

"Well, first of all," began Gnarstal, "each one of us is a magical being. We could just as easily have killed you before you landed and moved on. Plus, you had to have noticed that we just appeared here. If we wanted to cause problems, we could just as easily have appeared right beside Tanjork and struck him dead before anyone even realized what was happening."

Yeznull thought about this. She seemed to be very uncertain of what to do next. Sharnelle transformed into a dragon again, and stared at her. The gargoyle grew more nervous and looked around, as if planning the best means of escape. Finally, she sighed.

"I suppose you are correct," the gargoyle conceded. "Please follow me and I will lead you to Tanjork."

When they reached the castle, Kaylor, Sharnelle and Rirrom all shifted to human form, and the group entered. They were escorted to the throne room, where Tanjork waited for them. Yeznull nodded at Tanjork, and then left the room.

"So," said Tanjork. "You have something to tell me, I assume?"

"Yes," said Gnarstal. Then, he cleared his throat and explained everything that had happened since the release of the magic. It seemed to take a long time, and the only part that was left out was the encounter with Sylt. No one felt that this information should be told to these particular gargoyles. When he had finally finished, Gnarstal sat in a chair and waited for Tanjork to respond.

"Interesting," said the gargoyle. "If we could somehow convince the other gargoyles to agree to a truce, even if it was only long enough for the current crisis to be abated, then perhaps, in that time, we can get to know each other and decide not to continue the war at all."

"I never thought about it that way, but it is a very good idea. If we can just get the others to agree to such a truce..." said Reeflak.

"Very good," declared Tanjork as he clapped his hands together. "I'll leave it to you all to work out all of the details and return to me with the arrangements. Of course, you are all welcome to spend the night here at the castle tonight, as it is too late to worry about such things this night." He rang a bell that seemed to appear from nowhere, and a few other gargoyles hurried into the room. "See to my guests," Tanjork told them.

Chapter Twenty-One: Unicorns

Zanthorn was nothing short of terrified. He had made a tremendous error, and was now uncertain of how he should proceed. He couldn't just run away, because that would be even more suspicious than if he tried to play himself off as Acire. Fortunately, he had the advantage, as well as the added bonus of already knowing the name of the one who had addressed him.

"Majyk! I didn't know that you were here," he said, trying to change the subject. It worked!

"I just got back. I went to see if I could find your mother, but she has just vanished. I tried to follow her, but I was unable to use my magic to locate her. It is as if she no longer exists. Oh! I shouldn't have said that! She's your mother after all."

"No. It's okay. I would rather hear it from you than anyone else," said Zanthorn, really getting into his part. "However, you need to hurry and tell the herd stallion. I will be along in a moment, once I have come to terms with what you have just told me."

"Are you sure you will be okay?"

"I think so," replied Zanthorn. "I just need a moment to… To accept it all, I guess. But, the others need to know about this as quickly as possible. I can't let you be delayed because of me. I could never forgive myself."

"Of course. I will make my report and then wait for you. Do hurry," said Majyk as he walked away from Zanthorn and towards the rest of the herd. As soon as he was out of sight, Zanthorn shifted form again, becoming a roc. He flew up to the tallest branch that would support him. From there, he watched the herd. Having had dreams that he was a part of this herd had made the things he was seeing more understandable to him, as they did not communicate with regular speech.

By spying on the unicorns, he was able to discover several things. One thing that he learned was that there were humans on this world, and several of those humans had magical talents. He also discovered that the release of magic back on Htrae had started a chain of events that was now causing Htrae and Evol to slowly combine. The unicorns were concerned by the changes that had occurred because of the magic, and they were all convinced that this was the worst thing that could have happened. Zanthorn smiled to himself, knowing that this was definitely not the *worst* thing that could happen.

He decided that he had learned enough from the unicorns and so he took flight, going in search of humans. He was certain that the humans would be in need of a leader as they prepared to take over Htrae. He thought about how fortunate it was for them that he had stumbled into this world, as he believed he would make such a great leader for them. Soon, he would be able to show all of those who opposed him that he was even more powerful than they had ever been willing to believe he was.

Chapter Twenty-Two: Captive

In Sylt's dungeon, Shalon was waiting for the gargoyle to present himself. She was growing impatient. Using her Mindpower, she reached beyond the confines of the dungeon, seeking the leader of these gargoyles. In the rooms beyond the dungeon, she found seventy distinct minds. One was approaching her, and she was certain it was Sylt. She pulled her power back within herself, and then smiled as she waited for him to enter the room.

Sylt, acting even more self-important than he felt, casually walked into the dungeon and looked at his prisoner. His shock was so great, that he fell over once again. His throat constricted, and the scream he tried to release refused to come out. He was having trouble breathing as he scrambled backward. He came to the wall and used it to pull himself back to his feet. He had been expecting to find an elf in here. That is, after all, what his guards had said. Coming face to face with a dragon was the last thing he expected. He turned to run out of the dungeon.

"Wait!" cried Shalon as she reverted to her elf form. Sylt stopped, and turned to look at her. He was amazed by what he saw. He stepped back into the room and waited to hear what she had to say.

"Please help me," she begged. Then, for reasons she could not explain, she continued: "I don't know what is going on. I don't know exactly how it happened, but Zanthorn and I are no longer sharing this body. I don't know how I ended up back in this world. And, I certainly don't know what it is that I am supposed to do now!"

"Shalon?" asked Sylt. "Is that you?"

"How… How do you know my name?" queried Shalon.

"Your mother and uncle were here earlier tonight. They were here with two gnomes, a fairy, and a *unicorn*." He said the last word with evident disgust. "They tried to get me to help them save the world. However, I am at war with a rival clan of gargoyles, and cannot spare the time needed to help them."

"But, if you weren't at war?" asked Shalon, already forming a plan in her head.

"Well, then… I suppose I would have some time to spare."

"Even if the war was not actually over?" continued Shalon.

"What do you mean?" asked Sylt.

"I am talking about a truce. A temporary cease fire that will allow both sides to help us," explained Shalon.

"Well, I don't think that they will be willing to agree to that. And, even if they did… We have been at war for so long that I am not sure we would know how to treat each other."

"So, what if the war was to end?"

"Then, I suppose we would be forced to learn how to treat each other," said Sylt.

"I am curious about something," said Shalon. "Why is it that you are even at war?"

"Well," scoffed Sylt. "That is obvious! It has to be because... I mean, surely it is because... Uh... Well, perhaps it is because... Oh! I don't know!" he admitted.

"Hmmm. And, if you don't know," explained Shalon. "Then perhaps your enemies do not know, either. And, if that is the case, then it may be easier to end this war than I thought."

"I see what you mean. If no one knows why we are at war, then what is the point of continuing it. Very well. I will agree to end this war forever."

"Thank you, Sylt," said Shalon. By the look on the gargoyle's face, she knew she had made a mistake. She waited to see if he would give her a way to correct it.

"I have told you how I know your name," declared Sylt with obvious suspicion. "Now, will you please tell me how you came to know mine."

"Oh, well, the gargoyles who caught me stated that I was now the prisoner of Sylt. Therefore, I assumed that Sylt would be their leader. Since you are the only one who came to see me, I believed you were that leader. And, if you are their leader, then you must be Sylt. Simple logic, really," explained Shalon, glad that she had been given a way to explain it without having to tell him that she had used her Mindpower to invade his mind.

"You are very wise, Shalon," said Sylt, nodding. He was silent for a moment, and then continued: "So, if we are to go to Tanjork and request peace, we should be well rested. And, you cannot rest well in this dungeon. Come. We shall find you a comfortable room somewhere in the castle, and we shall head off to find Tanjork in the morning." Then, to himself he mumbled, "Though I don't know how much good it is going to do, since it won't bring back my son!"

Chapter Twenty-Three: Combination

During the night, while the creatures on both Evol and Htrae slept, their worlds combined. There was now a gray sky, in which three green moons and six purple moons could be seen. The trees became a darker shade of blue, while the leaves were still red and black, but had taken on a metallic sheen. The grass in this newly created world was both gray and amber, while the dirt became a paler shade of yellow. Clouds that had once been either maroon or yellow were now neon orange.

The combination of the geography was more complicated, however. Instead of having the geography of one world combine with that of the other, it was more as if someone had cut up two separate maps and combined them as one. Mountain ranges now divided what were once vast plains. Rivers flowed into seas that were no longer there. Large bodies of water now separated buildings that had been side-by-side only moments before. The only things that seemed to be unaffected by this combination were the creatures themselves.

Morning gave birth to a host of problems, as two suns – one aquamarine and the other a deep blue – rose over a landscape that its inhabitants had never seen before. Panic broke out across the land almost as quickly as the rays of the suns settled upon it. Most creatures were unable to explain what had happened, and none of them knew where to turn to find the answers.

"Oh, no!" screamed Rirrom when she had awakened. "This wasn't supposed to happen yet! I don't understand what could have caused it to happen so soon!"

"What do you mean?" asked Sharnelle.

"We knew that the worlds were going to combine, but we didn't know exactly when. We did know that it wasn't supposed to happen so soon. Acire said that we would have at least another week," explained the unicorn.

"This is so strange," said Kharn as he looked around.

"What a scholar!" bellowed Kaylor.

"This certainly complicates our mission," said Gnarstal. "We still need the help of Sylt if we are going to have a chance to defeat Zanthorn. The only difference now is that we must cover more ground in even less time."

They all agreed that Gnarstal was right. They decided that they would begin their trip to Sylt's castle as soon as they had finished their breakfast. After they had eaten, however, they discovered a new problem. None of them was certain where Sylt's castle was, in this newly created world. Finally, they decided that they would have to transport themselves to Sylt's castle using magic.

Chapter Twenty-Four: Plan

After working on the spell for a couple of minutes, the group believed that they had found a way to transport themselves all the way to Sylt's castle. Unfortunately, they did not accurately predict how much distance there was between them and the destination they wanted. The group appeared on a piece of land that, centaurs had inhabited when it was a part of Evol. Before they could be seen, they scrambled out of sight and discussed their next move. As it turned out, though, this was the best thing that could have happened, because Shalon and Sylt had similar plans, and had made the same mistake. They appeared, accompanied by a couple of guards, a few seconds after the first group had found their hiding place.

"Where are we?" asked Sylt.

"I have no idea. This doesn't look like any part of Htrae that I have ever seen before," said Shalon.

"You are on a piece of what used to be Evol," explained Rirrom. "In a centaur camp, to be specific."

Aber and Anitram, the two guards who had accompanied Sylt and Shalon, glared at Rirrom as she moved into view. However, they put their spears away when the rest of the group came out of the bushes to join her.

"Mother!" cried Shalon as she rushed to embrace Sharnelle. As the others watched this touching reunion, Rirrom turned away, trying to hide her tears.

"Shalon? What are you doing here?" asked Kaylor.

"Zanthorn is gone," Shalon told him. "I don't know what happened. I was getting tired, so I landed, shifted form and went to sleep. When I woke up, I was in another place. And, I was a dragon again. I couldn't find Zanthorn, and when I entered a cave, I was back in Htrae, where I was captured by gargoyles who took me to Sylt." She didn't bother to mention that she hadn't actually looked for Zanthorn.

"Zanthorn must be on the loose, then!" screamed Rirrom. "That must be what caused our worlds to become one. When Shalon and Zanthorn crossed over to Evol, it wouldn't accept the two minds in a single body. Zanthorn must have a new body!"

"And that means he also has renewed magic," explained Sharnelle. "We have to find him and destroy him before it is too late!"

"No!" cried Shalon. They all turned to face her. "We can't destroy him. We can only hope to defeat him."

"Great," sighed Gnarstal. "And, how can hope to accomplish that?"

"I have a plan," said Shalon. "Listen to this..."

Chapter Twenty-Five: Deal

Zanthorn took full advantage of the Combining. He used it, and the confusion it caused, to gain power. Within a few hours of sunrise, he had a human army practicing magic to use against the creatures of both worlds. He had been very careful about the way he spoke and acted, and as a result, over three thousand humans trusted him.

Shalon, in the guise of Temptra, appeared in front of Zanthorn. The magician, taken totally unawares, only stared in shock. Shalon, seizing the opportunity, grabbed Zanthorn and created a magical bubble around them, so that no one could interfere with her plan.

"Alright, Zanthorn," she told him. "Here's the deal. There will be no changes, and no repeating. Listen close. In exactly three days, we are declaring war on you. We are giving you time to find an army of your own, besides these humans. There is a rule, though. You may only recruit those who will follow you willingly. Whoever wins the war will have complete control of this world, and the other will be forced to surrender control. That's the deal. Any questions?"

"Why not just attack us now," asked Zanthorn.

"Because, unlike you, we want this whole thing to be as fair as possible. See you in three days!" she exclaimed just before she disappeared.

Zanthorn quickly went to work explaining things to those who were already part of his army. They all scattered to find any creatures that would be willing to serve Zanthorn. Two days later, the army returned to Zanthorn's fortress. Zanthorn was surprised to discover that his army of three thousand had turned into a group consisting of more than four and a half million creatures, including humans, elves, dwarves, gnomes, unicorns, ogres, giants, dragons, centaurs, gargoyles, harpies, and a few other creatures.

He spent the next day training his army, and was prepared to meet his adversaries when the time came.

Chapter Twenty-Six: Separation

When the time was up, Zanthorn found his army suddenly surrounded by the opposing army. He dismissed their chanting as a war song and began to give orders to his soldiers. Too late, he realized that his entire army was standing in a place that had been part of Evol while the opposing army was on land that was part of Htrae. The chanting that was coming from the other army was not a war song, but a complex spell. He hung his head in defeat, realizing that he had been defeated. Shalon had used him to get rid of not only him, but also all creatures that supported him.

Suddenly, it occurred to him that this was not entirely true. The spell was causing the worlds to split again, and all of the creatures that followed him were being sent to Evol, while the others were staying in Htrae. Now, he would have a world full of creatures that not only supported him, but who also viewed him as their leader. He could teach them to use their magic to its fullest potential without fear of anyone opposing his methods.

As the spell was completed, Shalon looked into her father's eyes and knew that he understood everything that was going on. She smiled sadly as all evidence of Htrae faded away and Htrae became the world she had always known. Then, she realized that it wasn't the same world. There were many differences, the largest being that the world now had a larger variety of creatures. As she considered the consequences of this, she was approached by a unicorn who shifted form.

"Shalon," said Acire. "I am Acire. I want to thank you for helping us."

"To be honest," admitted Shalon, "I wasn't doing it to help you. At least, not you specifically."

"Well, thanks anyway," Acire told her. "There is one thing we have been wondering, though."

"Oh?" asked Shalon. "What were you wondering?"

"Where did you get the idea for a second Separation?" the girl wanted to know.

"From Zanthorn, actually," Shalon said, laughing a little. "When the magic was set free on Htrae, and the two of us were trapped inside it, we went through all sorts of books, trying to find a way that we could escape. I saw the story of the first Separation and memorized the spell. I wasn't sure why I had done it at the time. When I discovered that the story was true, I decided to use that spell against Zanthorn and all of his supporters. Now, if you'll excuse me, there is something else that I must do."

"Of course," said Acire as she stepped out of the way. Shalon then walked past her and motioned to Sylt and Rirrom, who moved closer to her.

"That was a great plan," Sylt told her.

"Yes, it was most interesting," admitted Rirrom. Then, motioning to the girl with whom Shalon had just spoken, she added, "I see you have met my daughter."

"Yes, and what an interesting creature she is, too," said Shalon.

"What do you mean?" asked Rirrom.

"The Herd Stallion," replied Shalon, as if this answered the question.

"I don't understand," declared Rirrom.

"Look more closely at the Herd Stallion, Rirrom. You, too, Sylt. See anything unusual?" queried Shalon.

"Oh!" cried Rirrom. "I can't believe it!"

"What? You can't believe what?" demanded Sylt, who still had no idea what was going on.

"He's not a unicorn!" exclaimed Rirrom. "He's a gargoyle!" The Herd Stallion heard this, and approached. As he reached them, he transformed into his natural form. He was Sylt's son! Sylt stared in shock.

"I don't believe it!" Sylt cried. He stepped backwards, but when his son held out his hands, Sylt reached forward, taking his son into an embrace.

Shalon watched for a moment, then turned away. She walked to an open space and returned to her natural form. She spread her wings and took flight. Looking down from the air, she was surprised to see that the creatures were all getting along. Her mother and uncle joined her in flight. She looked at them and smiled.

"Let's go home," she told them. "I need to rest."

Epilogue

Shalon sat on the edge of a cliff, in human form, thinking about everything that had happened since her mother had been kidnapped. She couldn't believe how things had turned out. However, now that the magic was again split between two worlds and Zanthorn was no longer a problem for Htrae, she was certain that nothing like this would ever happen again. Strangely, the thought saddened her. Then she realized she was sad because she would never get to know Zanthorn, and he was, after all, her father.

Suddenly, she felt the presence of others. She turned around quickly. She discovered that Acire and Majyk were standing at the entrance to her lair. They looked uncertain of what they should do next.

"I'm over here," she told them. They jumped, then turned to face her. They walked over to her and shifted to human form.

"May we join you?" asked Acire.

"I don't see why not," Shalon told them. The two of them sat next to each other, a short distance from Shalon. Majyk nudged Acire in the ribs.

"Tell her," Majyk said.

"Tell me what?" asked Shalon.

"I. I was wondering if you would like to talk about your father," Acire said.

"You. You knew him?" Shalon wanted to know.

"Only through dreams," confessed Acire. "But I think I can tell you enough to satisfy your curiosity. He wasn't always evil, you know."

"Oh!" cried Shalon. "Of course I want to know!"

"You see, your father, Zanthorn..." began Acire.

www.ingramcontent.com/pod-product-compliance
Lightning Source LLC
Chambersburg PA
CBHW021127130626
46554CB00002B/890